Hey, Duck!

Carin Bramsen

SCHOLASTIC INC.

To Seets, with love and gratitude.
And to my sweetie, Gregg.

ISBN 978-1-338-03487-5

12 11 10 9 8 7 6 5 4 3 2 1   16 17 18 19 20 21

Printed in the U.S.A.   40

First Scholastic printing, March 2016

Hey, duck!

Why do you walk like that?

I slink because I am a cat.

Hey, duck!

    Why is your tail so long?

Oh, please don't call me **duck.**
It's wrong.

Now leave me
so that I can sup.

Hey, duck!

Don't get your
feathers up.

Such pretty feathers, by the way.

Such pretty fur, you mean to say.

Hey, duckie! Let's go play canoe,
and all the things that duck friends do.

We'll dance my favorite dance of all—
the **puddle stomp!**

We'll have a **ball!**

Oh, duck, why go off on your own?
We ducks can't stand to be alone.

Will you please note
that I'm a cat.
I want to be alone,
so
scat!

Who needs that grumpy duck for fun?

I'll do the
puddle stomp
for one.

I have my own canoe to float.

That poor old duck has
missed the boat.

Missed the boat? Missed the boat . . .

. . . Zzzzzz

MISSED THE BOAT!

Hey, duck?

That's not a duck.
That is a truck.

Hey, duck?

That's not a duck.
And just my luck.

Hello, my friend. You see I'm back.
And all I have to say is . . .

QUACK!

My sense of **me** has gone **amuck!**
I'm pretty sure I am a duck.
I'm **not** a cat, this much I know.
For no real cat would miss you so.

Oh, duckie dear! And I missed you!
Let's do the puddle stomp for **two!**

Uh-oh. Could I still be a cat?
I did not like that wet kersplat.

Well, duck or cat, you're my friend now,
which makes me want to shout . . .

MEOW!